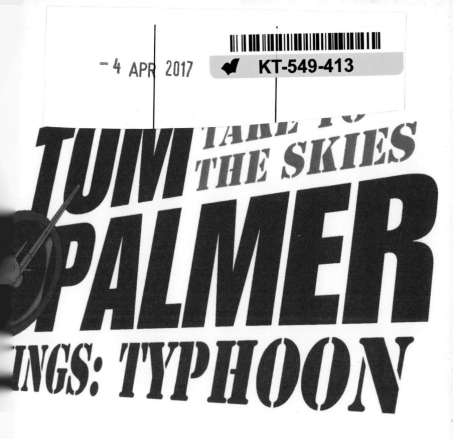

TOM TAKE TO
THE SKIES
PALMER
WINGS: TYPHOON

WITH ILLUSTRATIONS BY
DAVID SHEPHARD

First published in 2016 in Great Britain by
Barrington Stoke Ltd
18 Walker Street, Edinburgh, EH3 7LP

www.barringtonstoke.co.uk

Text © 2016 Tom Palmer
Illustrations © 2016 David Shephard

A CIP catalogue record for this book is available
from the British Library upon request

ISBN: 978-1-78112-537-3

Printed in China by Leo

For Iris

ONE

Jess was just about to play the perfect pass to her sister, Maddie, when a boom like thunder tore the sky in two. She ducked, fell over and could only watch as the ball rolled over the line, off the pitch and towards the changing rooms.

What the hell was *that*?

Jess had no idea. She was still on the ground, and when she dared to look up she saw the fiery afterburners of a war plane disappear into the perfect blue sky. The plane answered her question. The ear-splitting roar was one of the downsides of playing football on a pitch right next to an RAF air base.

"What sort of a pass was that?" Maddie yelled, as she strode towards Jess.

Jess hung her head. "The plane put me off," she said.

Jess could cope with almost anything that life on the football pitch could throw at her. She could get up after a foul. She could work on her game after a bad match. She could smile and shake hands after her team lost to another. Anything. But she could not put up with Maddie tearing into her in front of everyone else. Her sister never knew when to shut up.

"You're rubbish, Jess," Maddie yelled. "Total rubbish. We had time for one or two more attacks. Now we've got no chance of winning. And it's all your fault."

Jess knew better than to say anything. Instead she closed her eyes, dug her hands into the grass and ripped up two clumps of soft turf in silent rage. When she opened her eyes she saw that Jatinder had crouched down next to her.

"Your sister is a total hot-head," Jatinder said. "That plane's designed to scare the hell out of trained soldiers. Don't feel bad that it did the same to you."

Jatinder stood up and offered Jess his hand. She took it and let him haul her up.

"Thanks," she said with a smile.

Jess liked Jatinder. He was calm and a good footballer, but he felt like more than just a team mate. He and Jess and Maddie and another player, Greg, were staying with a couple in an old building called Trenchard House near the RAF base. They'd made friends right away – on and off the pitch – in the first few days of the football summer school. And now this was the last game before the school finished.

The last game and very nearly the last minute. The last chance to make an impression. It was time for Jess to forget her mistake, ignore her sister and get stuck in again.

Jess worked hard to win the ball back from the throw-in she'd given away. Before long, she put in a low sliding tackle, taking the ball off a dawdling defender. She played a neat pass to Maddie, who turned fast and dribbled the ball over to the far side of the penalty area.

Jess sprinted into the box, staying onside. Just.

"Maddie!" she called. "Pass!"

Maddie did her best to lose the defender who was forcing her wide. She turned, then hit a shot from a tight angle. Her attempt had plenty of power behind it, but went well wide. Soon after, the ref blew the final whistle.

Jess felt full of a hot, fierce anger. If Maddie had played her in they could have scored, got a draw. But Maddie was like that. Selfish. She never gave back to her team mates. She was too hungry for glory for herself. And Maddie didn't have the excuse of a war plane putting her off.

Jess glared at Maddie as they walked off the pitch.

Why did it have to be like this? They used to pass to each other all the time. They used to spend hours kicking a ball back and forth to each other in the garden, in the playground and on the beach on holiday. But those easy times together were a thing of the past now. Now Maddie thought she was something special because she'd started at secondary school. Whenever she was with Jess, Maddie made sure to treat her younger sister as if she was a baby.

After Jess had showered and changed, she met Jatinder and Greg outside the changing rooms. As they waited for Maddie, Jess looked for the last time at the mural of footballers painted along the low wall of the block in bright, bold colours.

"Come on," Greg said. "Let's get back to Trenchard House. We don't want to be late."

Jess nodded. She didn't want to be late either. Steve and Esther, who'd been looking after them, had promised that if they all behaved well they'd get a treat on their last day.

"Where's your sister?" Jatinder asked.

Jess shrugged, feeling her hair straggle wet against her neck.

"Is she still getting changed?" Greg said.

"Suppose so."

"Can't you go and tell her we'll be late?" Jatinder said, clearly getting fed-up.

Jess sighed. "Look. If I go in there and ask her to hurry up she'll just be slower on purpose. We'd be better just to wait."

Jatinder gave her a funny look. "Really?"

"Really," Jess said. "Haven't you noticed that when I ask her anything she either refuses, does the opposite or just ignores me?"

Jess saw Greg and Jatinder share a confused look.

"If she doesn't get a move on," Greg said, "we'll be late back to Steve and Esther's and we'll miss the treat, whatever it is."

TWO

Even on a clear, sunny day like today, Trenchard House was old and spooky. But Jess thought it spooky in an exciting way, not scary. And there was a reason for that.

When they first arrived, they got a tour from Esther and Steve, whose house it was. Esther had explained that the house was where fighter pilots had stayed during the First and Second World Wars. She'd showed them all the framed photos on the walls and told them that these airmen had flown missions from the old airfield near by.

"They were brilliant, fearless men," Esther said. "Heroes. But far too many of them never came back from their missions."

"See this guy?" Steve said, and he pointed one pilot out. "He's from St Kitts in the Caribbean, like my dad. He's even got the same name as him – Basil. Which makes him almost like family in my book ..."

Connections. History. That's what Jess liked about the house. There was history in the wood panels in the hall and in the creaking floorboards. Jess could sense that those brave airmen had once slept in the same rooms as they were now, eaten their meals at the same table.

It turned out their treat was a trip to an air show that was taking place today at the RAF base. As she waited for the others to get ready for the air show, Jess looked at the faces of the old pilots and a question came into her mind.

"Esther?" she called.

"Yes, Jess?"

"Why are there no photos of women?"

"Good question," Esther said. "The truth is, I don't know. We looked through all the boxes we found in the attic, but couldn't find any photos of female pilots."

"Didn't women fly in the wars?"

"Not in the First World War – as far as we know – but they did in the Second," Esther said. "Even then they didn't fly in combat like they do now. But they moved the planes around, sometimes from country to country. It was dangerous work. They must have been great pilots."

Jess looked at Esther, then back at the old black and white photos. She was amazed.

"You know," Esther went on. "I sometimes look at the pilots' faces and wonder if they really were all men. See this one? Doesn't the face look almost female? There were rumours that some women knew how to fly and were desperate to fight, and so they pretended to be men so they could join the RAF."

At first Jess thought Esther was joking, but then she saw that her face was serious. Jess turned back to the faces of the pilots, looking more carefully now. *Could* any of them be women? There were plenty with moustaches and beards, and most of them seemed to have men's strong, broad faces. But the one Esther had pointed out could almost be a woman, if you looked closely.

Esther sighed. "Where have the others got to?" she said. "The air show will be over before we get there. I'll tell them to get their skates on."

Esther ran up the stairs, leaving Jess on her own. Jess stared harder at the face of the pilot again. There was something different about the chin and eyebrows. Something troubled but defiant.

As Jess looked into the pilot's eyes, she sensed colours flashing just out of her vision. She turned round, expecting to see that the hall light was flickering. But the light wasn't even on.

Then Jess felt a rush of air push past her. And a sudden weight in her legs and arms that made her want to sit down. Her vision flashed dark and she wondered if she was going to faint.

What was happening to her?

She sat on the bottom step of the stairs, leaned forwards and took deep, steady breaths. She was about to put her head between her knees, as she'd learned to do if she felt faint,

but then Esther's husband Steve came into the hall.

"You OK, Jess?" he said.

"Bit dizzy," she replied. She still felt wobbly and confused.

"It'll be the excitement," Steve joked. His eye's were shining and it was clear he was the one who was excited. "I love air shows," he said. "They're awesome!" Then he looked at Jess again and registered that she really wasn't feeling well. "Come on," he said. "Let's get you a glass of water."

Jess followed Steve into the kitchen where the air was brighter and cooler. The tap gushed as he filled a glass with water, then he went over to the freezer to find some ice for her. The radio was on, with the news blaring out.

"Sit and drink this," Steve said. "I'm going to see what the others are doing."

Jess drank her water and listened to the news.

There was some awful stand-off going on in North Africa. A journalist reported that a group of terrorists was threatening to murder hundreds of innocent people. The United Nations had called on the government of the war-torn country to protect its citizens. The reporter went on to say that the RAF had sent six fighter jets out to Cyprus, on standby to fly south and help prevent the massacre. The jets were ready to take action that evening, the journalist added.

Jess frowned as she thought about the plane that had stormed across the skies over the pitch earlier that day. She thought about the photos on the wall, and the RAF pilots flying from their base in Cyprus tonight. Would any of them be women?

THREE

A silver bi-plane was floating like a kite above the entrance to the air show when Steve and Esther, Greg, Jatinder, Maddie and Jess got there at last. A big grey plane swooped past the bi-plane, then disappeared into the high cloud overhead.

Security guards in hi-vis jackets checked Steve's backpack before they were allowed into the show.

Once they were in, Jess stayed close to the two adults. The place was packed and she didn't like crowds. She could see the tops of stalls selling T-shirts, balloons, model planes and all sorts of other gifts. She could smell frying onions and hot dogs, candyfloss and an odd oily smell like petrol. The roar of planes' engines was deafening.

Jess wished her mum and dad were there. They knew that she hated crowds, and they would know that she would find everything here a bit much. Her dad would find her something to focus on, to distract her from the crowds and the noise. There was no way she could expect Steve and Esther to understand.

Jess looked at Maddie in the hope that she would remember her fear of crowds, but Maddie was too busy craning her neck, looking for something. Jess had no idea what.

Suddenly Greg grabbed Jess's arm and pointed towards a plane moving high in the air above them.

"Spitfire! Spitfire!" he yelled.

Jess looked at Greg and realised he could barely speak. She saw tears in his eyes.

"Are you OK?" she asked. She didn't have a clue how to read his weird behaviour.

"More than OK." Greg beamed at her. "It's amazing. I love it. Look at that – a real Spitfire."

Jess felt better as she looked up at the curved wings of the old plane. She didn't know quite why Greg was so happy, but his happiness made her feel happy too.

Now she felt calmer, she could look around and take it all in. The air show was split into three zones. There was a field of tents with displays and activities. Then there was a runway zone packed with planes and helicopters, and thousands of people admiring them. Last, there was a huge expanse of open fields with nobody in it, just planes flying above.

All of a sudden, Maddie was there, grabbing Jess by the arm and moving her away from Greg. "Look!" she said. "Look!"

"Ouch!" Jess pulled her arm back. "What is it, Maddie?"

"Come on. Please. Look!"

A "please" from Maddie was as good as a "sorry" and so Jess looked. Maddie had spotted two clean-shaven young men in black flying suits and dark sunglasses. Next to them were two women wearing exactly the same uniform as the men, their expressions equally serious and focused.

"So?" Jess said. "Who are they?"

"Why do you always have to ask me stupid questions?" Maddie snapped. "Isn't it obvious?"

"No."

"Two pilots. They're amazing, aren't they?"

"Four," Jess said, looking again at the two women next to the men. "Two men," she said. "Two women. Four pilots."

"Women don't fly proper planes," Maddie said.

Jatinder and Greg had just come over and Jess was trying to work out if her sister was winding her up when a low rumbling noise grew and grew until it became so deafening that Jess had to put her hands over her ears. A compact grey plane rushed over the crest of a low hill, then turned to shoot directly up into the sky. As it rocketed upwards, Jess could see two points of red at the back of the tail.

Like everyone else in the crowd, the four football school kids stood and stared.

"It's a Typhoon," Jatinder shouted over the din. "The RAF's best fighter aircraft. Isn't it awesome?"

Jess nodded. She didn't know if she'd call it awesome, but she was stunned. The noise of the plane was making the inside of her chest vibrate. She felt like all her senses were under attack.

But, to her surprise, she realised that she was loving the rush of adrenaline racing through her. She took her hands off her ears, then looked at Maddie, who stood gawping too.

Jess grinned at her. "It's like the one we saw this morning," she said.

"*What?*" Maddie yelled.

"This morning. When I missed my pass. It's the same kind of plane." Jess smiled, trying to make light of earlier.

But Maddie just turned away.

Jess felt the adrenaline drain from her body as the noise of the Typhoon faded. She wished she could read her sister better. Sometimes Maddie wanted to talk to Jess, to be with her. Sometimes she didn't. And Jess felt that she could never get it right.

Then Jatinder was shouting. "Look! A flight simulator. And there's almost no one in the queue. Steve! Esther! Can we, *please?*"

Esther looked at each of them in turn. Greg and Jess were nodding and Jatinder was hopping up and down in excitement. Maddie shrugged like she was too good for it all.

"OK, kids," Esther said. "Let's give it a go."

Jess and Maddie followed the others in the direction of an oval-shaped pod perched in the field like a space ship from an old sci-fi film. It was the size of a large car, but higher off the ground, with a set of steps up one side. The famous RAF roundel, a big red dot inside a blue circle, stood out on the pod's smooth silver surface.

"Come on then," Maddie said. "If we have to."

FOUR

When the summer school group arrived, the door of the simulator was rising, like a bird lifting a single wing. A dozen people emerged and stumbled down the metal steps, grinning and chatting, blending with the streams of people walking around the air show. Jess took their happy faces as a good sign. Perhaps this make-believe ride in a Typhoon would be exciting after all.

Jatinder and Greg joined the queue. Then Jess. Maddie stood behind Jess, still aloof from them all.

A young woman checked their tickets. As she looked up at Jess, Jess felt a jolt of recognition. She looked really familiar. Something to do with the spark in her hazel eyes. Jess was sure she'd seen her before – but where?

"This is the last ride today," the woman said. She hung a chain across the back of the queue. "OK?"

"OK," Jess said. "But will we all get in?"

"Of course," the woman said.

"But there are fourteen of us in the queue," Jess said. "And that sign says it only seats twelve."

Then there was that roar of sound again, blocking out the conversation. The low-flying Typhoon rattling the air all around them.

Jess covered her ears to escape the storm of noise and again she felt the vibration of the plane's engines deep inside her body.

Then she shook with another feeling. It was like the way she'd felt at Trenchard House when she'd looked at the photo of the pilot she thought might be a woman. As if her arms and legs were suddenly heavy, an odd feeling of weight on her shoulders and in her chest. She put her hand on a rail to steady herself as a stream of light and colour rushed past her at high speed.

It was weird and it was confusing.

Jess noticed Maddie holding onto the rail too. "Are you OK?" she asked.

"Yeah." Maddie smiled a shaky smile.

"But do you feel that?" Jess asked her.

"Feel what?"

"I don't know."

Maddie's smile turned into a snarl. "For God's sake, Jess. Will you stop asking me questions? Save them for –"

"Come on," Greg said, interrupting Maddie's rant. "We're in."

Jess watched the people ahead of them showing their tickets and then filing into the simulator. Greg and Jatinder were last.

Jatinder turned round as he climbed in. "Oh ... it's full," he said.

"Full?" Jess said. "But ..."

Jess looked at the woman on the desk as she pulled a lever to shut the simulator door. On the last ride of the day.

"I can't believe it," Maddie muttered. "That's so not fair."

Maddie glared hard at the woman as she hit the button to set the simulator running.

"OK, girls." The woman sighed. "Don't look so worried. You two can go in on your own after this lot. OK?"

"Great," Jess said. "Thanks."

Maddie remained silent. She said "thank you" almost as often as she said "sorry" or "please".

The two girls watched the simulator pod as it jerked and rattled. Jess grinned at Maddie. But the grin died as soon as she noticed the uneasy look on her sister's face.

Maddie's pale, anxious face reminded Jess that her sister had her own fears. Not crowds like Jess – Maddie was scared of small spaces.

Jess remembered how one summer they'd gone on a ghost train with their mum and dad, squashed up together in a tiny little wagon, and Maddie had lost it. The ghosts weren't a problem – she'd lost her nerve in the tiny space, so badly that their mum had to hit the emergency button to stop the ride.

No one spoke about it afterwards and Jess had never mentioned it to Maddie. She knew her sister was embarrassed that she had lost her nerve when Jess hadn't.

Jess wanted to ask Maddie if she felt OK now – and if she'd seen the strange blazes of light and colour a few moments ago. But there was no way of knowing if Maddie would flare up at her again, so she left her concerns unspoken. She could feel that Maddie was bristling with tension and she didn't want to make things any worse.

Six minutes later, the hydraulics hissed and the door of the pod swung open.

Jess saw Jatinder first. Then Greg.

"How was it?" she asked.

"Good," Greg said. But Jess could tell by his voice that it had been a bit of a let-down.

"Where did you fly to?" she asked.

"The Lake District," he said. "The Welsh mountains. Green fields. No cities."

"Come on. Jump in, girls," the woman interrupted. "Before anyone else wants a go. Sharpish. I should be finished by now – I've got a class to teach later."

Jess climbed in first. There were four benches one behind the next, each with a silver handrail. Jess chose to sit on the front seat, right up against the screen. She left room for Maddie beside her.

But Maddie climbed in behind her and sat two seats back.

Jess looked down. The actual space between the two of them wasn't so big, but she had never felt so distant from her sister.

FIVE

To distract herself from her sister's snub, Jess scanned the inside of the simulator pod. The wide seats. The big screen. The three red buttons on the ceiling.

She turned to Maddie. "Look," she said with a grin. "Buttons for the ejector seats. In case we crash."

But Maddie didn't laugh at Jess's joke. She had that face on that she sometimes wore now. Jess tried to work it out. It wasn't a grumpy face or a superior face.

What was it exactly?

Then Jess knew. It was Maddie's nervous face. Her sister was nervous, even scared.

The door began to close, the bright sunshine of the day outside fading to a gloom. Then darkness.

"I didn't even want to come on this stupid ride," Maddie grumbled. "It's for kids. I'm only doing it to keep you company."

Jess was about to tell Maddie that she knew she was scared. But she bit her tongue. She knew it was best to leave her sister to it. This was no time to push her.

"Thanks," Jess said in a cool voice, then she turned to face the front where the screen flickered on in the dark.

There was a pilot on the screen. He was walking along a runway explaining what was going to happen next. "I'm taking you on a journey," he said. "A journey full of thrills. But, in the event of an emergency, you must hit the red button above your heads."

Then the screen showed the sharp-pointed nose of a plane as it sped down a long strip of runway. Seconds later they were in the air. Green fields replaced white lines and smooth concrete as the plane climbed into the clouds. It didn't just look like they were flying – it felt like it too. The pod juddered and shook, moving with the motion of the screen.

'Fab!' Jess thought. But she sensed that Maddie thought it was far from fab. Jess heard her swear under her breath and looked round to see her clutching the rail in front of her, staring straight ahead with her teeth clenched.

Jess couldn't ignore her sister's distress any longer.

"It's all right, Maddie," she said. "It's just pretend."

As soon as the words were out her mouth, she knew she'd made a mistake.

"I don't need you to tell me it's OK," Maddie shouted, her face like thunder. "I know it's OK. I know it's pretend. I'm older than you. I know more than you. So shut your face, OK?"

Stunned by the fury of her sister's harsh words, Jess turned back to stare at the screen. Normally she would have loved the wild scenery and wide open spaces as the plane flew through mountains and valleys and swept over lakes. But she couldn't enjoy it because she was crying. Big, silent sobs.

She'd only been trying to comfort Maddie. What had she said that was so bad?

Why was everything she said and did always so bad in Maddie's eyes?

And why was Maddie always so grumpy? Always trying to make out she was better than

Jess? She was never nice. Never just Jess's sister like she used to be when they'd kick a ball about together.

Then Jess was hit by that strange gravity thing again. She felt heavy, so heavy. As if something was dragging her down to the floor, all the organs in her body pushing her backwards.

Was Maddie feeling the same way?

Did they both have some kind of awful virus or something?

Jess had no idea. All she could do was stare at the screen as they sped faster and faster over the hills and valleys. The landscapes turned green, then grey, then yellow, as if they were flying over some empty wasteland, not the fields of England and Wales. The colours were like the flashing lights at the edges of her vision that she had seen at Trenchard House.

They were the colours of sky and clouds and desert rushing past them.

The movement of the pod was different now. The juddering had stopped and the ride felt smoother, faster. And the pod itself had changed inside. Now it was all lit up like the cockpit of a proper plane.

Jess looked down and gasped. The wooden benches were gone. In their place were narrow canvas seats like a pilot would sit in. Jess was strapped into hers, facing forward. The silver handrail had gone.

There was a hi-tech control stick and a panel of buttons and switches right between Jess's knees.

Jess breathed out and gazed around, utterly bewildered. What on earth was going on?

She had no idea. All she knew was that none of it felt right.

In fact, it felt terrifying. Very terrifying and very wrong.

SIX

"Maddie!" Jess shouted, twisting her body to see behind her. "Maddieeeee!"

For some reason Jess couldn't see or move her head properly, and it took a lot of effort to turn round to look at her big sister. But Maddie wasn't there. Instead, a stranger looked back at her – a stranger in a silver helmet with a dark visor. The visor reflected the huge sky back at Jess – and her own reflection, in an identical helmet.

The stranger was a pilot, just like the four pilots at the air show.

Jess knew she wasn't in the simulator pod any more. She was in the cockpit of a fighter plane.

But how could that be? They'd got into a ride for kids. They hadn't taken off in a real plane.

Then Jess remembered what Greg had told her as he came out of the simulator. The views that he'd seen had all been of green valleys and lakes. There was nothing green or blue to be seen here. Just miles and miles of blank, sun-bleached desert.

Jess stared at the control stick in front of her. She reached out a hand to touch it and was shocked to see that she had big green gloves on.

Gloves? Control stick? Helmet? Visor? *Desert?*

She needed to know what was going on.

42

Jess's hands felt bulky in their gloves as they hovered over the stick. What would happen if she touched it? Could she actually control this thing? Whatever it was?

She had to find out.

Jess put her hands round the control stick and breathed in. She moved her arms carefully and slowly, drawing the stick towards herself. The movement tipped the cockpit towards the sky, and the ground beneath them dropped sharply away.

Jess swallowed.

"MADDIE!" she shouted. "Maddie, I need you."

At last Jess heard Maddie's voice. But it wasn't her normal voice. It was a quiet, electronic version of her voice and it was coming through the headphones that Jess was wearing.

Headphones? Where had they come from?

That was *Maddie* behind her in the silver helmet?

This was all far too weird.

"Stop moving the simulator," Maddie begged. "Just leave it, OK?"

"We're not *in* the simulator," Jess said. "Something's happened. Something's gone wrong."

"Don't be an idiot." Maddie's words sounded strangled. "What are we in, then? A plane?" Her voice was controlled, but Jess knew that it was the control of someone in a panic who was trying hard not to fall apart.

Jess tried to control her own breathing so she could speak, so she could think. Maddie was right. Of course she was. Jess was an idiot to think they were in a plane. She twisted again to see Maddie, to see her sister's face. She knew Maddie's eyes would tell her what mood she was in. Her eyes would tell her if she meant what she said.

But of course all Jess could see was the helmet, the dark visor and the dramatic, silvery reflection of sky and desert.

"Oh, Jess." Maddie's voice was shaky now, but sarcastic. "You're *so* lame. Where else could we be but in the simulator? Thank God this ride finishes soon. Then I can get away from you and back to the other idiot kids."

Jess couldn't let it go this time. This was so far from right. Jess *had* to challenge her sister, even if Maddie flared up at her.

"If I'm so lame, then why are you wearing a helmet, Maddie?" she demanded. "And why am I wearing gloves? And why can we see behind us now? There was only a screen ahead of us when we got into the pod." Jess felt herself getting more and more wound up, so she paused for breath, then went on. "And why is a red light flashing on my screen to tell me we're out of fuel?"

Jess stopped and screwed her eyes shut for a few seconds. Her breath was too short and shallow to speak any more. Her heart was pounding. And now she could see something ahead. A black dot. There was something up there in the sky with them!

Jess pulled the control stick back to ease the plane upwards, level with the black dot.

"I said, leave that stick alone," Maddie growled. "And stop asking me your *lame* questions."

Jess ignored her. "What's that black dot in the sky ahead of us?" she asked. "And how come I know how to control this plane?"

Jess waited in the hope that Maddie would answer. She needed answers. She would even be happy if her sister could somehow prove that she was an actual, real-life idiot and they really were still in the simulator pod. At least then this nightmare would end.

But Maddie said nothing and all Jess could hear was the eerie electric whine that passed for silence in the cockpit of their Typhoon.

SEVEN

The black dot in the sky was getting bigger and bigger.

What was it?

And, more to the point, what was it going to do to them?

It was all too much for Jess. She felt sick with fear and panic. Her hands were frozen on the control stick and she was staring ahead, unblinking. That was it. She wasn't going to move again until this was all over. She wasn't going to be here in this cockpit. That was how she would cope.

Jess sat as still as a statue made from ice. Doing nothing worked – for a minute. But the black dot was getting closer.

"What is it?" Maddie said at last.

Jess didn't reply.

"What is it?" her sister asked again, her voice urgent.

Now that Jess could see the dot more clearly, she knew that it was a large plane. It was getting closer and closer. Soon it would reach them and whatever was going to happen would happen and all of this would be over.

Jess wanted it over. As long as she did nothing it would happen. And, however bad it was, it would bring this nightmare to an end.

Then Maddie's voice came through Jess's headphones.

"Four-two to base. Status please?" Maddie said.

"Base to four-two," an electronic voice came back. "Progress to refuel before onwards to target."

"What!" Jess said. "Maddie, what are you talking about?"

"I'm trying to get us out of this," Maddie said, and she sounded focused and in charge. "We need to do something. I'm sorry. You were right."

"No," Jess said, and her voice cracked.

"Yes," Maddie replied.

"Mum," Jess moaned. "I want Mum."

"I know," Maddie said. "But Mum's not here. We can do this, Jess. You and me together.

Move the control stick down. Go on. Move the control stick again. I know you can do it."

"Do what?"

"Refuel."

"No way," Jess said. "I'm not moving."

"Yes you are. You have to. If we don't refuel we'll crash very soon."

Jess shook her head.

"Please, Jess," Maddie said. "I need you to do it, Jess."

The plane ahead of them wasn't a black dot any more. It was wide grey wings, a sharp tail and a long, sleek body.

Jess closed her eyes, then opened them again. Maddie was right. She had to listen to Maddie. She had to act. She gripped the control stick and moved it, bringing them ever closer to the giant plane.

"Good, Jess. That's really good," Maddie said. "Now, line the pipe up."

A thick tube appeared right next to the front of the plane's canopy.

"What is it?" Jess asked.

"A fuel pipe," Maddie said. "It's where the fuel goes in."

"You are kidding." Jess groaned and covered her face with her hands.

"Come on, Jess," Maddie said. "You can do it. I've seen you do loads of things when you thought you couldn't. Remember when we went on that tree-tops rope walk? It was so high up

and so unsteady, I froze. But you were fab. You swung across, no bother at all, even though you were the youngest there. And half the boys chickened out, like I did. But not you."

Jess remembered all right. But it felt good hearing about it from Maddie. She hadn't mentioned it before.

They were almost touching the giant plane now. Its massive grey hulk was blocking out the sun.

"Go on, Jess," Maddie said again. "You can do it. I know you can."

Jess knew full well that Maddie was trying to make her feel better so that she would get on with flying the Typhoon. That was why she had started to talk to her this way. And Jess realised she didn't mind. She liked having her sister in control – it felt right. Her sister was older. It felt fine.

Jess heard herself say, "Maybe I can, but Maddie ... when you spoke to that person before – the base – what did it all mean?"

"I don't know," Maddie said. "Which bit?"

"When the base said we had to refuel before we advanced towards our target," Jess said. "But what target? Maddie, what's our target?"

EIGHT

Jess moved the control stick to keep their plane in line with the pipe hanging from the back of the massive grey tanker plane. Somehow she knew to edge them closer and closer, until their nozzle linked up with the fuel line.

It took two or three attempts, pushing forwards, then dropping back again, before Jess got it right.

As soon as the two planes were connected, Jess saw the red fuel light on the control panel flicker off. OK, so they weren't going to crash from lack of fuel now. That was one good thing. That and the fact that her sister was being nice.

But the connection with the tanker plane and the connection with her sister weren't enough for Jess. The word *target* was still spinning round and round in her mind. What did it mean?

Jess's mind ran wild with thoughts of what a war plane like this one might have as its target.

They had seen a Typhoon at the air show, and Steve had told her that the planes carried nothing but weaponry. Bombs. Missiles. Cannons. A targeting pod. That's what this plane – this Typhoon – was for. It was built for combat. It was designed to destroy.

"Maddie, what is the target?" Jess asked again.

"I don't know, Jess," Maddie almost snapped. "Let's focus on refuelling. Let's think about targets when we need to."

"But ..."

"But nothing, Jess."

Jess felt her eyes go hot with tears. "But we've almost finished refuelling," she said, her throat tight. "The target is the *next bit*. We're in a plane flying faster than 1,000 miles per hour and we're going to bomb something. And then, once we've dropped our bomb, other planes will attack. They'll attack *us*! I've seen it on the news."

Jess's speech was met with silence from Maddie. A long silence that filled Jess with an overwhelming fear that she might suffocate. It seemed that, this time, Maddie might not have an answer.

Then Maddie spoke ...

"Look, we've worked out how to fly this plane," she said, calm as anything. "And how to refuel it. I don't know how this is happening – or why – and maybe it's a dream, or maybe it's real. But we have to do what we're asked to do, like real pilots. We advance to the target. We drop whatever we have to drop. Then we'll be instructed to fly back home. They'll show us where to land and then we'll be out of this. We don't have any choice. Do you understand?"

No, Jess didn't understand. Her heart was racing with panic and she couldn't think straight. And her heartbeat sped up even faster when she saw the refuelling pipe come away and fold back into the wing of the tanker plane.

Then that electronic voice spoke to her again.

"Base to four-two. Confirm refuel complete?"

"Four-two to base. Confirmed."

"Four-two. Advance to target. You have your co-ordinates. The target must be destroyed. Understood?"

"Understood," Maddie repeated in a clipped, military voice.

"Understood?" Jess yelled at her sister. "You *understand*? You know how to destroy a *target*? A target means people – we'll be destroying *people*."

"Yes, I understand. I know what to do," Maddie told her. "And the target isn't people – it's a store for weapons, an arms store for terrorists. If we don't bomb it they'll use those weapons to murder people."

Maddie's words horrified Jess. She wasn't worried now that they didn't know what they were doing in the plane. It appeared that they did know. What horrified her was the talk of bombs and destruction.

"I know what you're thinking," Maddie said.

"Do you?" Jess snapped. "What's that then?"

"You're worried about bombing the arms store. You think it's wrong. But remember the news this morning? The RAF have intelligence on a planned attack, and they know where the terrorists are storing their weapons. If they can hit the store before the attack, then we'll save thousands of lives."

Jess did remember. And she did – kind of – understand. But she didn't understand why she and her sister had to do this. She'd never signed up to destroy anything. Her eyes flicked from symbol to symbol on her screen. Something had changed. But what?

And then she saw.

A map. Green digits. Co-ordinates for the target. That's what had changed.

Jess knew exactly what the lights and symbols meant.

"Maddie?" she said, trying to sound calm.

61

"Yes?" There was a familiar hint of irritation in her sister's voice. A hint of the old Maddie, letting her little sister know just how much she got on her nerves.

"It says here ..." Jess said. "It says on my screen that our target is only four minutes away."

NINE

High in the sky and four minutes from their target.

Jess jangled with nerves. She felt vulnerable, an easy target. They were in a Typhoon and about to fly smack into a war zone. They were the target now. A deadly burst of missiles and bullets would shoot at them from the ground. What would happen if they were hit?

As Jess thought, the answer came to her in a bold, clear flash. They had to go down, right down. She had to fly this plane as low as she could. And fast. Jess had no idea how she knew that was the right thing to do. But it *was* the right thing, the only option.

Jess pushed the control stick forwards, slow and firm. The Typhoon tilted, pitching down at a steep, sharp angle.

The force of the tilt pushed Jess back in her seat. *Whooah!*

It was almost like being in a rollercoaster at the point when it tips over the top and you start to plummet to the ground. Except there was no track to keep them on course. They were falling out of the sky. Jess felt the pressure in her body, as if all her blood was surging into her head.

"What's going on?" she heard Maddie snap. There was nothing of the calm older sister in her voice.

"I'm taking us down," Jess said.

"What? Why?" Maddie demanded. "Are we out of fuel? Have we been hit?"

"No," Jess replied though her headset. "I've decided to take us down to 20 metres."

"What?" Maddie shouted. "Are you crazy?"

"No. It's what needs to be done. So I'm doing it. Sit tight."

Jess turned her focus back to flying the plane. The level of focus needed was draining her fast. Using the controls took a huge effort, but that was nothing compared to the effect of the forces on her body. She could feel her flying suit pushing hard against her. It was a really weird feeling, almost like the suit was a heavy weight, pressing into her of its own accord.

Jess stared out of the cockpit and saw the desert floor speeding closer and closer. She could see features on the ground now. Tracks or dry river beds. Clusters of low, twisted trees, spread far apart. And vehicles – trucks, lorries and rugged four-by-fours.

"Jess, take the plane back up," Maddie shouted. "We're just about on top of them. They can see us. They'll shoot us down."

"The nearer we are to the ground the less chance they have of hitting us," Jess told her.

"What? Don't be stupid. Fly higher. Now."

"No – you have to trust me."

"Just do it," Maddie snapped. "I order you to do it. I'm the oldest. I'm in charge."

"Maddie, listen to me ..."

"Do it. Now. JESS! Listen to me –"

"I am listening to you," Jess snapped back. "But you're not listening to me. And you need to. I'm not going to change what I'm doing."

Maddie was silent for a few seconds. Jess moved the control stick back to take some of the sharpness out of their descent.

Then Maddie spoke. "OK," she said, her voice low. "Tell me."

Jess levelled the Typhoon. She could see the surface of the desert as it rushed beneath them, really close and really fast. It was beyond amazing. But that didn't matter. What mattered was that she knew she was doing the right thing. They were scarily close to the missiles that could fire at them from the ground, but they were much safer down here than up in the sky.

"The higher we are, the easier it is to see us coming," Jess explained, her voice wobbling. "Up high, they can take aim, fire at us. If we come in low, they won't see us until the last second and by the time they aim at us, we'll be a mile away. We're travelling at incredible speeds – more than 1,000 m.p.h. At 20 metres we're just a blur to anyone on the ground."

Jess held her breath, waiting for Maddie to reply. They needed to agree on this. She kept the Typhoon level, even though she was desperate to fly lower. She knew she needed to take the plane even further down to take them out of the line of fire.

"OK," Maddie said at last. "You've convinced me. Fly as low as you like."

TEN

Jess could feel her heart pounding inside her flying suit. Her legs and arms were braced, clenched hard as she focused on flying the plane low over a desert road at a phenomenal speed. A speed so fast that she had to fight to breathe. A speed that had her teetering on the edge of panic.

But, despite her terror, Jess knew her plan was working. And that sensation of doing the right thing was amazing. Now she felt more than fear.

Excitement.

Elation.

Joy.

It was an incredible mix. Jess felt like she was on fire.

But then she saw bright flashes from the desert floor. The flashes flared like matches just struck, or sparks from a firework. They were intense and sudden like explosions, but Jess could hear nothing except the almost silent electric whine inside the cockpit.

"What was *that*?" Maddie asked, her words distorted by the headset.

"Enemy fire," Jess said. "But it's OK. We're low. They won't hit us."

"Go back up," Maddie demanded again.

"Maddie," Jess told her sister. "We're here to bomb an arms store. Remember? That's what you said we had to do. We're here to save people's lives."

Then there was a noise Jess had never heard before. A noise that made her heart race. Maddie was wailing – a wail of pure despair and fear.

"I don't want anyone to depend on us," Maddie wailed. "Not here. Not now. I want to go home. I want Mum and Dad ..."

Jess stared straight ahead through the glass canopy at the yellows, greys and browns of the desert floor. She stared at the flashes from the road, the flashes from weapons trying to shoot them down.

And, behind her, Maddie had cracked, just like Jess had cracked before. She wasn't confident or in control any more. She was howling.

Jess could feel hot, unhappy tears spill down her own cheeks inside her helmet. Without Maddie as her big sister she was broken too. What should she do? Crash land the Typhoon into the desert and hope they'd wake from this terrible nightmare? Fulfil their mission – drop the bomb, destroy the arms store, save innocent lives?

"Maddie?" she said, at last. "I need you. I can't do this without you. I don't know if we should fly up or down or if I should just close my eyes, scream and hope for the best. You're my sister and I need you. I want Mum and Dad too, but you said it before. They're not here and we haven't got a clue what we're doing –"

Then Jess heard herself scream as a sudden flash burst in front of the cockpit. A blazing red and orange streak hurtled into the sky. She saw her hands rigid on the control stick but she felt powerless to move them.

A missile had almost hit them.

It was far too close.

Then two more flashes. One from under the sharp point of the left wing of the Typhoon. One from under the right wing.

Jess watched in horror as another fiery flash rose to meet it, and the sky ahead of them exploded into shards of grey and black and white.

"What was that?" she shouted.

"Me." It was Maddie's voice, steady again now.

"What?"

"I fired a set of flares. Someone on the ground is firing heat-seeking missiles at our engines. The flares confuse the missiles. They draw the fire. Stop us getting hit."

Jess breathed out. She hadn't realised she'd been holding her breath.

"How did you do that?" she gasped.

"I hit a button. I just knew what to do. Like you said. And, Jess?"

"Yes?" Jess said, delighted her sister was calm and in control again.

"We're less than two minutes away from the arms store. As soon as we reach it, the bomb drops, then you get us out of there? OK? We can do this. Together."

ELEVEN

Jess could see the arms store.

She didn't need to monitor her screen to check their approach – she could see it through the curve of the cockpit window. First, a low mountain range came into view. At its base there was something that stood out in the endless yellow-grey desert. Something that grew bigger and bigger as they flew towards it at 25 miles a minute.

There it was – the arms store. It was shaped like a spider's web etched into the ground.

"I see it," Jess told Maddie.

"I have it on the screen," Maddie confirmed. "Seventy seconds."

"OK. So, I keep the plane level and then you drop it?" Jess asked.

"No. The bomb drops automatically. It's programmed. You do what you're doing and when the timer hits zero the bomb drops."

"Then what?"

"Just focus on getting this bit right. We stay steady, keep the plane level. We reach the target. The bomb drops."

"Yes, but then what? What happens after that?" Sweat was pouring off Jess and she felt waves of panic hit her again.

"You'll know what to do, Jess," Maddie said. "I know you will. I'm here if you need me."

Jess smiled, and it helped her to keep a grip on her fears. Her sister trusted her. That was good to know.

"Thirty seconds," Maddie said, jolting Jess back into the moment.

Jess stared straight ahead. She saw flares down below – more incoming fire. But no one would hit them now. She was 20 metres above the desert. Anybody down on the ground would be ducking and covering their ears as the Typhoon screamed across the sky.

"Twenty seconds."

Jess prepared herself. Ready to lift the Typhoon away from the explosion. Ready to take the plane back up into the skies. The Typhoon would move up and to the left, she knew that much. And Maddie's faith in her made her feel sure that they'd be OK. She didn't need to ask any more questions.

"Ten seconds."

A light flashed on Jess's screen and she watched the ten short pulses. Each one a second apart, although it felt like a minute or more. Then the timer showed zero.

Jess pushed the throttle forward to slow the plane down and tipped it a little to the right.

Ahead of her, she saw the bomb as it hurtled fast towards to the arms store.

For a second Jess couldn't take her eyes off it, but then she shook her head. 'Forget the bomb,' she told herself. *'Forget it.'*

She had to get her and Maddie away from the explosion. The bomb from the Typhoon was about to explode, and so were all the bombs, missiles and other explosives in the arms store. The blast would be enormous.

In one sharp, swift movement, Jess moved the control stick back and to the left.

Then she eased the throttle forward and the thrust of it threw her back into her seat. The sense of force and power was extraordinary. She could barely see. Her head was full of a searing heat. Nothing made sense, and yet Jess was aware that the desert floor was disappearing fast.

The Typhoon was climbing at speed.

There was a flash. White. Red. Orange.

It was blinding. It was far too bright.

Jess closed her eyes and turned her head away as she took the Typhoon higher, twisting it in a tight 180-degree turn.

Three or four seconds later, Jess tipped the plane's wing to look down at the arms store.

They had hit their target.

No question.

The intensity of the blast was incredible as thousands – maybe tens of thousands – of bombs and missiles exploded. Anyone near the arms store would have been blown to bits. The thought horrified Jess, but she told herself that if she hadn't destroyed this target, its firepower would have been used to kill hundreds of innocent people.

She looked down again, and the image seared into her mind.

"You did it, little sis," Jess heard Maddie say through her headphones.

The sky was bright behind them. It felt as if the sun was rising after the darkest of nights.

"*We* did it," Jess replied. "Big sis. Now we just need to get home."

"Home," Maddie echoed.

Jess checked her screens. Everything looked good. She focused on making sure the Typhoon was heading in the right direction. Back home.

But now she had time to worry.

Were they really going home?

Who would she be when she got there?

And what about Maddie? Who would she be? Would either of them ever be the same again?

TWELVE

With her head full of questions and her heart aching, Jess tilted the plane higher and higher to speed away from the explosions that were destroying the terrorists' arms store.

Both girls were quiet as they climbed. It was impossible to speak. The force of the plane as it sped upwards had them pinned to their seats. It felt to Jess like the pressure in the cockpit was ten times stronger.

And then those feelings tilted into a memory. A memory of being back at Trenchard House. That strange feeling of being heavy, of having to hold onto the stair rail to steady herself. The stream of colours flashing out past the corners of her eyes.

"This is just like at the house," Maddie said, as if speaking Jess's own thoughts for her.

"What?" Jess said, her mind fuzzy and blurred like she'd just woken up.

"That feeling," Maddie said. "It's just like we both felt in the house and at the air show. It is, isn't it?"

A tingle thrummed through Jess. It felt good to know that her sister was thinking the same thoughts as her, that they were still on the same wavelength.

"Let's hope we get back there," Jess said.

"We will," Maddie said.

"Sure?" Jess asked.

"Yep, I'm sure." Jess could sense the smile in Maddie's voice. "This whole thing is really weird. But if you can fly us back to wherever we're supposed to go, then we'll be OK."

Jess levelled the plane out and pushed the throttle forward. If what her sister had said was true, then she wanted to make it happen as soon as possible. She looked down from the cockpit to the sea ahead of them, a sparkle of blue beyond the dull yellow of the desert. In the distance, across the water, there was a small island jutting out from the sea.

"Jess?" Maddie said.

"Yeah?"

"I'm sorry."

"What for?"

"You know."

Jess said nothing for a few seconds. What could she say?

"It's OK," she said at last, in a squeak. "Me too."

"I miss being at the same school as you," Maddie said. "And I don't like secondary school much. It's made me act funny."

"You've been OK," Jess told her.

"Not really," Maddie said.

"Well, I've been funny with you too," Jess admitted. "I don't know what it's like to start at a new school. I could have been nicer to you. I could have made it easier."

"Maybe," Maddie said. "But we're OK now, aren't we?"

"Yeah," Jess said, grinning inside her helmet. "We're more than OK."

They flew on, the sun going down. An orange and blue haze burned ahead of them, and the great black shadow of night grew behind them.

Jess pushed the control stick forward and the Typhoon pitched down.

"Jess!" Maddie yelled. "What are you doing?"

"Everything's fine," Jess said. "We're going to land soon."

"And are you OK about landing?" Maddie asked.

"Of course," Jess said. "You told me it'd be OK – remember?"

Maddie didn't answer.

Jess waited.

"It *will* be OK," Maddie said. "Do what you think is right. You've done so much already. It'll be fine. I trust you."

Jess could see the outline of the island clearly now. A shape in the middle of the sea, a bit like a swordfish. That was where they had to land.

THIRTEEN

As Jess guided the Typhoon down to the island, then onto the smooth surface of the runway, she checked the screens, made sense of the co-ordinates tracking the plane's progress, pushed buttons and used the control stick as if she was an expert, trained for years to do just that.

And she felt completely calm and focused. None of it came as any surprise to her. But what happened next did surprise her.

Maddie came to sit next to her, and she put her arm around Jess's shoulder.

"Good job," Maddie said.

Jess grinned. "Thanks," she said, leaning into her sister's body.

Then the screen in front of the girls went black. A list of names scrolled upwards, like the credits at the end of a film. Jess and Maddie sat reading them, in shocked silence.

"Eh?" Jess said. "We're in the simulator pod again. Now what?"

"I don't know," Maddie replied.

Then, a moment later, the door began to rise. Light streamed in as it opened. They were back at the air show.

The woman who had taken their tickets stood waiting as they climbed out, unsteady and unsure.

"How was that, girls?" she asked them with a smile.

"Great, thanks," Maddie and Jess said together.

"And how did you get on?" the woman asked.

"We got on really well," Maddie replied.

"No problems?"

"No problems."

"Great," she said, still grinning. "See you. I'm off to my class now."

The two girls walked away. Jess glanced back at the woman, but she had turned away from them. She wanted a proper look at her – her face was so familiar, but Jess still couldn't remember who she reminded her of.

The air show was quieter now. No planes in the sky. Just a scattering of people. But there was their group from the football school, waiting for them.

"Come on," Jess heard Esther say. "That's us finished for today. The show's nearly over."

Jatinder and Greg grumbled a bit, but soon they were walking towards the big white tent at the exit. As they left the simulator behind, Jess's mind made the connection.

The woman in charge of the simulator.

Jess knew who she looked like. It was the old photo of the pilot on the wall at Trenchard House. The man with the troubled, defiant look. The man who might be a woman. It was her.

Jess gasped and looked round, but the woman was gone. Nothing remained of her but a strange hum in the air, a distorted blur of shadow.

*

Esther drove them all back to the front gates of the football school, where Greg and Jatinder's parents would be waiting.

Jess and Maddie's mum was coming later. Esther had told them that an emergency at work had held her up.

As they drove, Steve switched the radio on. "I want to hear the news," he said. "I need to know what's happening."

Esther sighed and drummed her fingers on the steering wheel. But she stopped and listened, just like they all did, when the news came on.

The first story was about North Africa. British planes had joined French and American forces in bombing raids on key terrorist arms stores. The single RAF Typhoon involved had returned safely to land in Cyprus. The strike had destroyed the terrorist group's firepower and the town under threat of attack was safe.

Jess clapped her hands together and caught Maddie's eye. Her sister looked pale, but she was smiling.

"I didn't think you were that interested," Steve said, twisting round in his seat.

"Well, we are," Maddie said.

"Yeah," Jess agreed. "We're interested."

Esther parked outside the football school, and Jatinder and Greg said goodbye. There were smiles, jokes and laughter. Hugs and promises to stay in touch. Then car doors slammed shut, engines started up and the boys waved as they drove off.

Then Jess and Maddie went back to Trenchard House for the last time.

Jess stood at the foot of the stairs as Maddie finished packing her bag, taking twice as long as she really needed, like always. Jess was studying the old photo of the Second World War pilot. Could it be a woman?

The more she looked, the more Jess felt sure. It *was* her. It was the woman from the air show. The look in those eyes was unmistakable.

Thump ... thump ... thump!

Maddie dragged her bag down the stairs and came to stand next to Jess, interrupting her thoughts.

Jess pointed at the photo on the wall.

"Look at that pilot's face," Jess said. "It looks familiar. Does it remind you of anyone?"

Maddie put the ball she was carrying down and squinted at the photo. A pause of concentration – and then she shook her head.

"No," she said. "Anyway, Mum's just texted me."

"Is she nearly here yet?" Jess felt a rush of excitement. She had missed her mum, and her dad.

"They'll still be another hour," Maddie said. "Traffic's terrible, she says."

"Oh," Jess said, and the rush of excitement vanished as quickly as it had arrived. "Oh well."

"So." Maddie tossed the ball to Jess. "Fancy a kickabout while we wait?"

"You sure?"

"Yeah, come on." Maddie beamed at Jess, then gave her a playful dig in the side. "Let's work on those skills – you and me together, sister!"

Maddie and Jess dribbled the ball between them as they ran towards an open piece of ground that marked the start of the old runway.

Esther and Steve sat on the front step of the house and watched the sisters as they kicked the ball in short, focused passes to each other.

The sun was low now, shining orange through the trees. The air seemed to glow, almost hum with golden light.

"The airfield looks magical just now," Esther said, as she leaned into her husband's side.

Steve nodded and pulled her close. Esther was right. "Magical indeed," he said. "For us, for our old wartime pilots and for those two footballers out there now."

For Steve felt sure there was something magical about the airfield every night. And he hoped there always would be.

ABOUT TYPHOON

The story of *Typhoon* begins in the pod of an ordinary flight simulator that turns into a real Eurofighter Typhoon.

I had the idea for this book after I'd been in a Typhoon flight simulator with my daughter at an Agricultural Show. First we looked at some prize chickens and then we experienced what it might feel like to fly a Typhoon. Our experience didn't turn into anything more 'real-life', of course. But at many times and places, women have flown aircraft into war.

In the Soviet Air Force in the Second World War, there was a whole regiment of female fighter pilots called the 588th Night Bombers.

The situation was very different in the UK.

Between 1918 and 1920, women could join the Women's Royal Air Force (WRAF). The plan was to train women as mechanics to help with Air Force work.

In 1939, at the start of the Second World War, the WRAF started up again as the WAAF – the Women's Auxiliary Air Force.

The women of the WAAF could not fly into "the theatre of war", but their role was to deliver planes where they were needed, including the front line. Women flew 300,000 planes into war zones between 1939 and 1945. And they flew them in skies full of enemy aircraft.

One in every ten of those women died. Just like their male counterparts, they were brave, skilful and determined to do what was needed to win the war.

It took until 1991 for a woman pilot in the RAF to fly into a war zone with a direct part to play in war. That pilot was Flight Lieutenant Julie Ann Gibson.

Then, in 1994, Flight Lieutenant Jo Salter broke new ground by becoming the first female fast jet pilot. She was a "combat ready" pilot who flew Tornados similar to the jet in this book and carried out bombing missions in Afghanistan and Iraq.

All this nearly 80 years after warfare in the air began.

I read about dozens of female pilots when I was writing *Typhoon*.

One woman's bravery really stood out for me. She was Flight Lieutenant Michelle Goodman, a helicopter pilot.

In Iraq, in the early hours of 1st June 2007, Goodman was woken by an urgent call-out – a British soldier had been badly injured in a major attack in Basra City. The soldier had to be rescued and brought back to the base within 15 minutes. If the rescue took any longer than that, the soldier would die.

Goodman took off from her base and flew her helicopter into the war zone. She landed her helicopter under fire and in a dust storm. As she landed she let off flares to confuse the enemy missile tracking systems, to prevent them from hitting her. Even so, the helicopter was hit, but Goodman took off with the injured soldier on board, and returned to the British Field Hospital.

Goodman carried out the whole mission at high speed – it took her just 14 minutes. The soldier lived – because Flight Lieutenant Goodman put her own life at risk to save his. She was awarded the Distinguished Flying Cross for her actions. She was the first – and so far the only – woman to be awarded this medal.

Men and women are still not fully equal in the Royal Air Force. Women can serve in combat roles in the air but they can't fight with the RAF Regiment on the ground. What do you think about that?

TOM PALMER

ACKNOWLEDGEMENTS

Without my daughter, Iris, I would never have written this Wings trilogy. It just wouldn't have happened. Full stop. When she was younger, we made plane kits together and when she was a bit older, we went on a Typhoon simulator together. It's at times like those that ideas for new books come to me. That's why I have dedicated this book to Iris.

But I needed more than just an idea. I needed to research *Typhoon*. And so I read stacks of books about modern warfare in the air in order to develop my ideas. The best of these books was *Tornado Down* by John Peters and John Nichol. Peters and Nichol were shot down over enemy territory and captured in the desert during the Gulf War, an ordeal that brought them close to death. Their account is a remarkable one, and I'd like to thank the authors for their honesty and bravery, and for what they were willing to do to serve their country. I would also like to thank the RAF and the RAF Museums, who inspired me and gave me support as I tried to get my facts right for all three Wings books.

As always I would like to thank my wife, my agent, David Luxton, and my publisher, Barrington Stoke. Thank you.